Six Men

First published in the United States by North-South Books Inc., an imprint of NordSüd Verlag AG,
CH-8005 Zürich, Switzerland.
Distributed in the United States by North-South Books Inc., New York 10017.

Library of Congress Cataloging-in-Publication Data is available.
Printed in Germany by Grafisches Centrum Cuno GmbH & Co. KG, 39240 Calbe, June 2011

ISBN: 978-0-7358-4050-8 (trade edition)
1 3 5 7 9 • 10 8 6 4 2
ISBN: 978-0-7358-4056-0 (paperback edition)
1 3 5 7 9 • 10 8 6 4 2

www.northsouth.com

DAVID MCKEE

SIX MEN

NorthSouth
New York / London

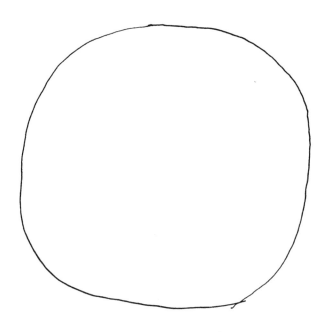

Once upon a time there were six men
who traveled the world
searching for a place
where they might live and work in peace.

At last they found the land they longed for.
There they settled down to build and farm.
And to their surprise, they began to grow rich.

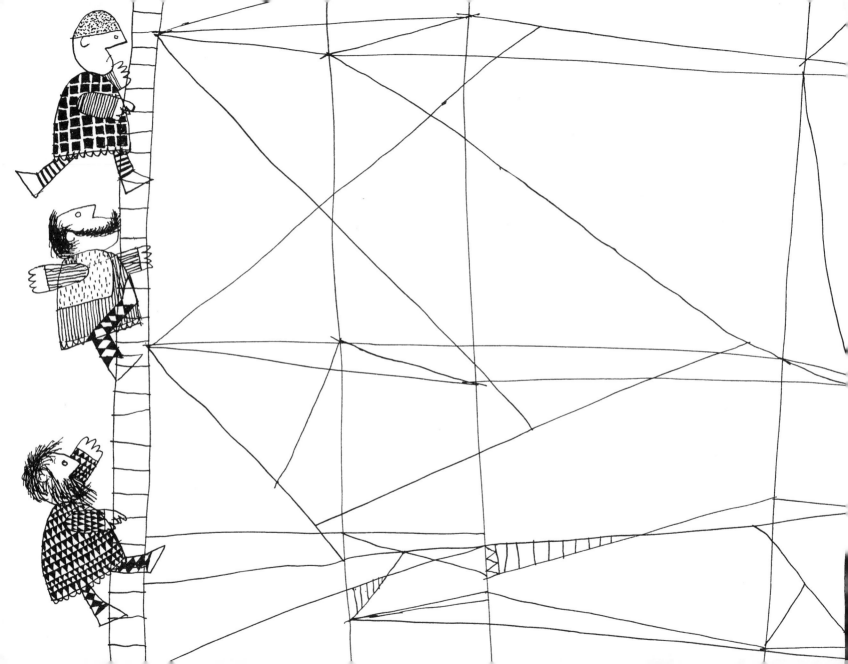

But as their riches grew,
so their worries grew.
They worried that thieves would come
and catch them unaware
and steal their wealth.
And as time went on,
they couldn`t work for watching.

So they built a high tower
that looked out across their land.
But then the six men spent most of their time
leaping up the ladder to watch for strangers.

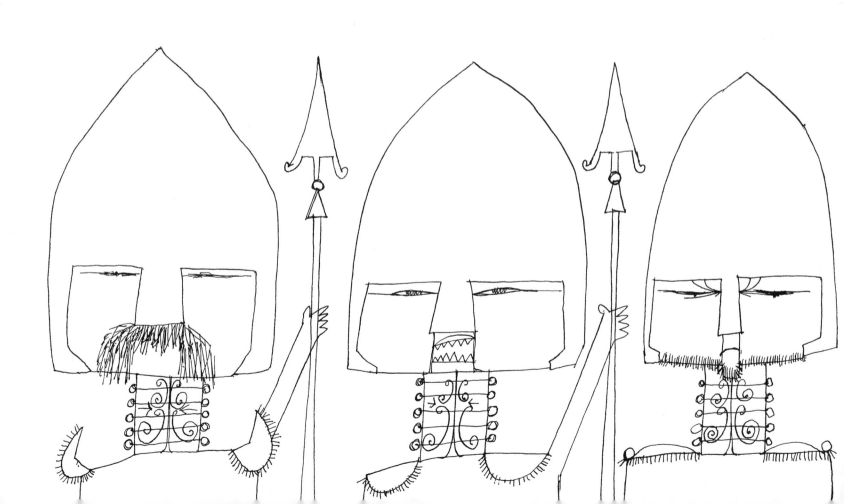

They decided to hire six strong soldiers
to stand guard in case of trouble.

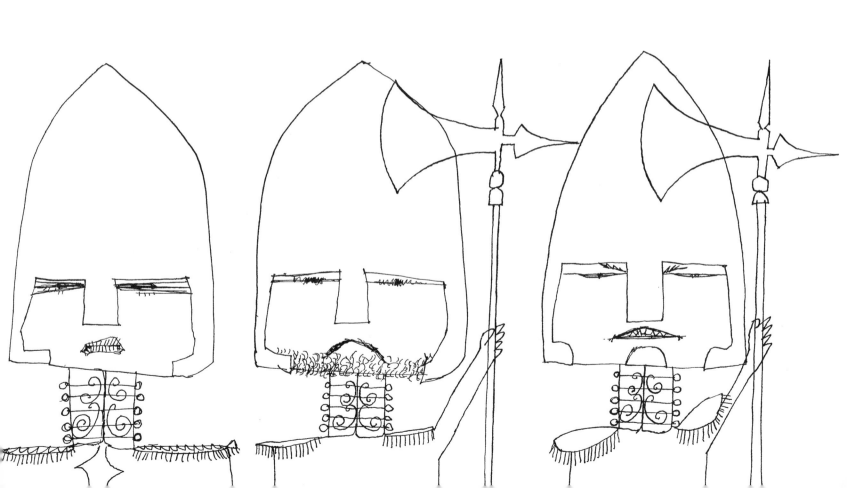

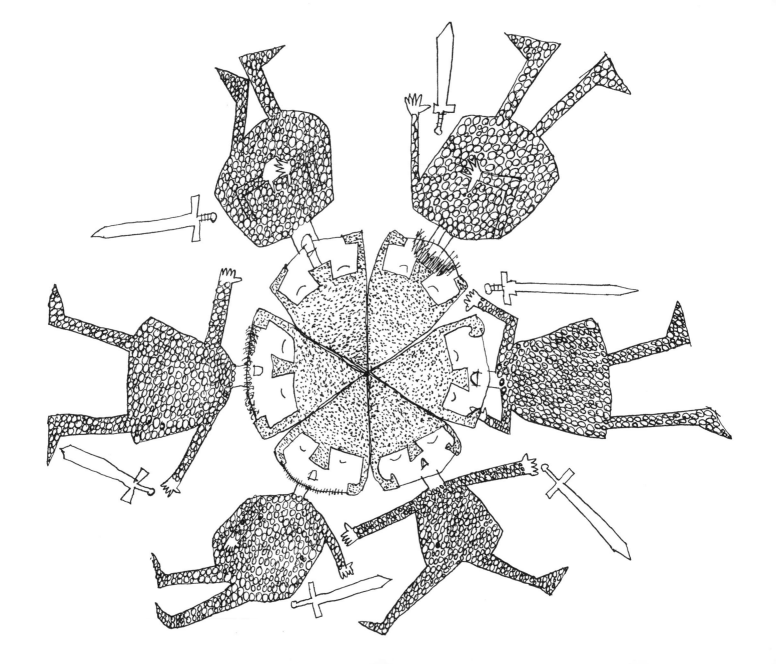

But no robbers came to rob,
and the soldiers grew fat and lazy
with nothing to do.

So the six men started to worry again.
They worried that the soldiers
would forget how to fight,
and they worried about the waste of their money,
and they decided to make the soldiers earn their keep.

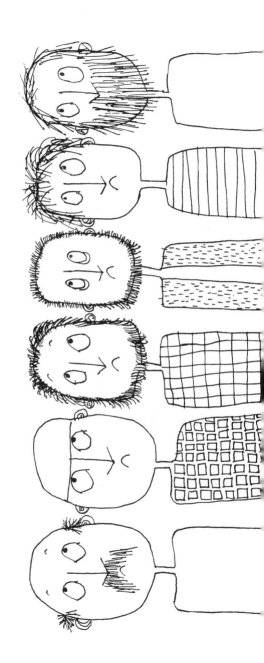

Next door was another farm,
and the six men thought it would be just the thing
for the six soldiers to capture.
It was easy.
The peaceful, friendly people who lived on the farm
simply took fright,
threw down their tools, and ran away.

Then the six soldiers marched proudly home,
and the six men rubbed their hands,
stopped worrying,
and started to feel strong and powerful.

They soon grew to like this feeling of power,
and the soldiers were sent to capture other farms.

Sometimes the farmers would hand over their land
and agree, in fear, to work for the six men.
But some of the farmers put up a fight,
and they were killed.

So the six men soon owned more and more land,
and they grew ever richer,
and they needed more and more soldiers
until at last they had a fine brave army
with the first six recruits as captains.

Their greed grew and their power grew
until the six men ruled over all the land
from the high watch tower
down to the great river.

Some of the farmers had escaped across the river.
There people still worked and lived happily together.

But when these people heard about the six men,
they began to worry too.

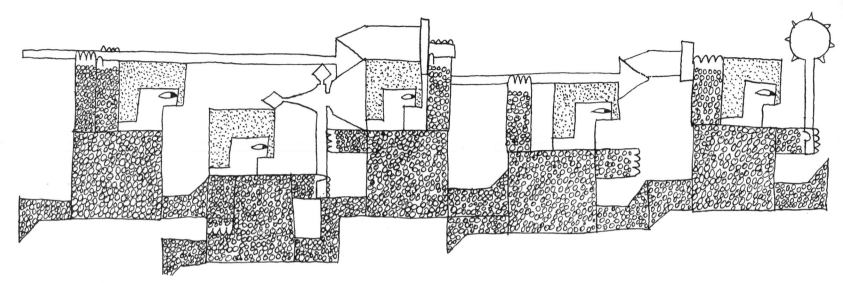

So they met together to make a plan.

They all agreed to form two equal groups.

Each group took turns, working as farmers for half their time
and training as soldiers for the other half.

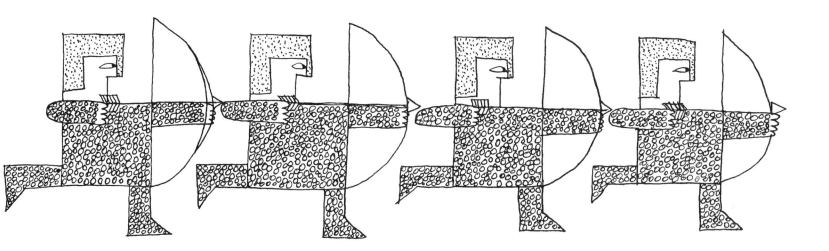

In this way they became well prepared to face an enemy.

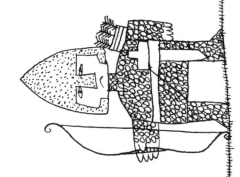

The six men mounted a guard on their riverbank . . .

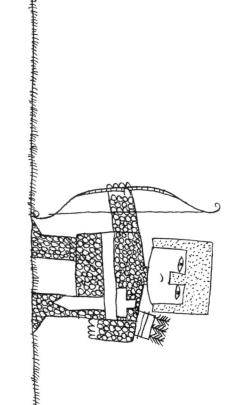

and on the other side the farming soldiers did the same.

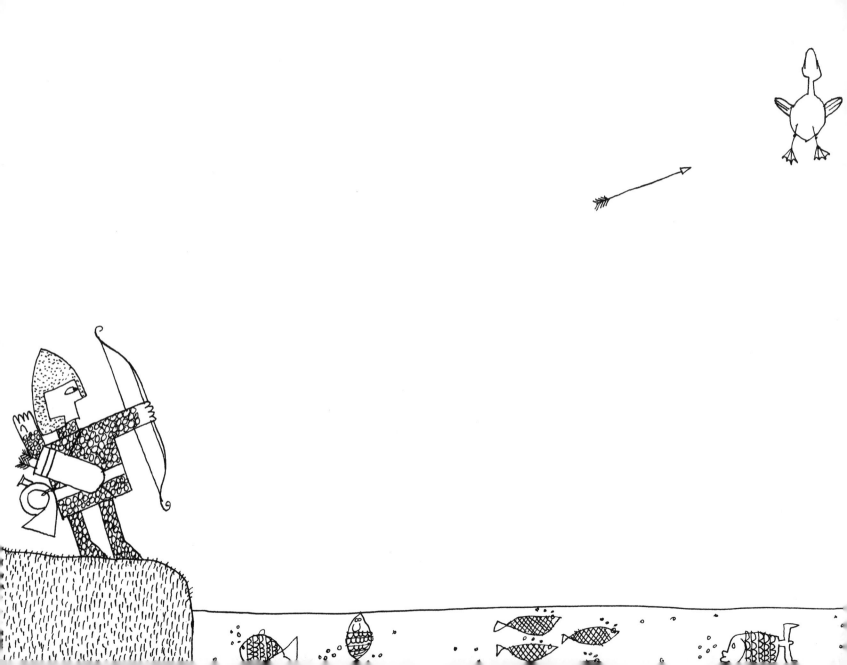

Time passed and all was quiet,
and the guards grew bored with nothing to do.

Until one day a little duck flew by.
Both guards saw it,
both guards fired,
and both guards missed.

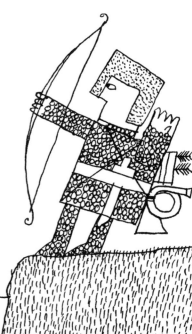

But the arrows crossed the river,
and each guard,
sure that he was being attacked,
sounded the alarm.

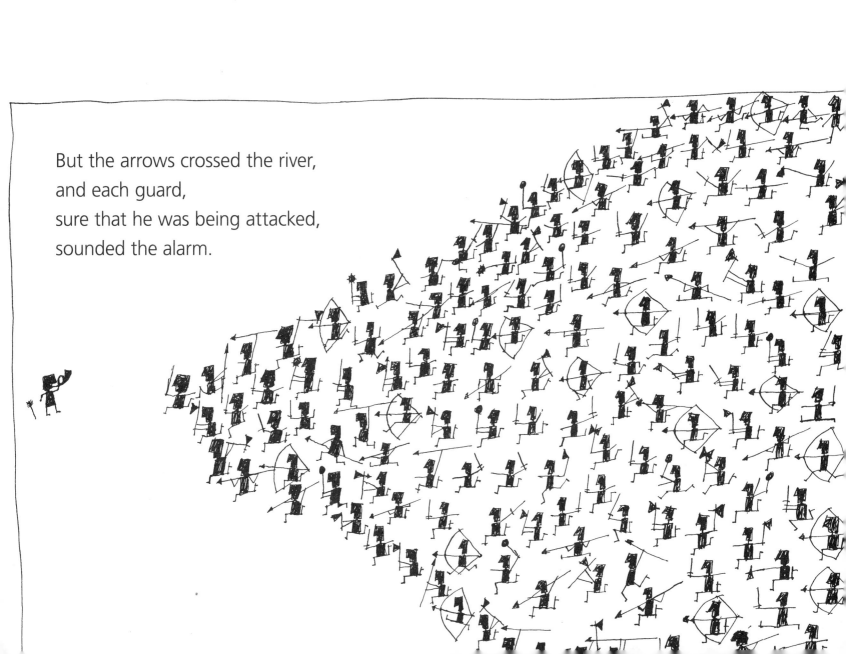

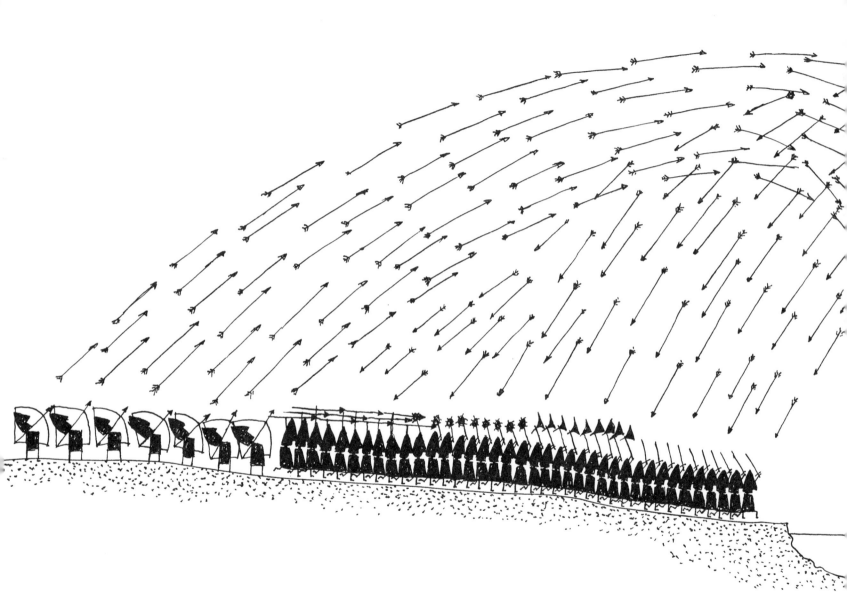

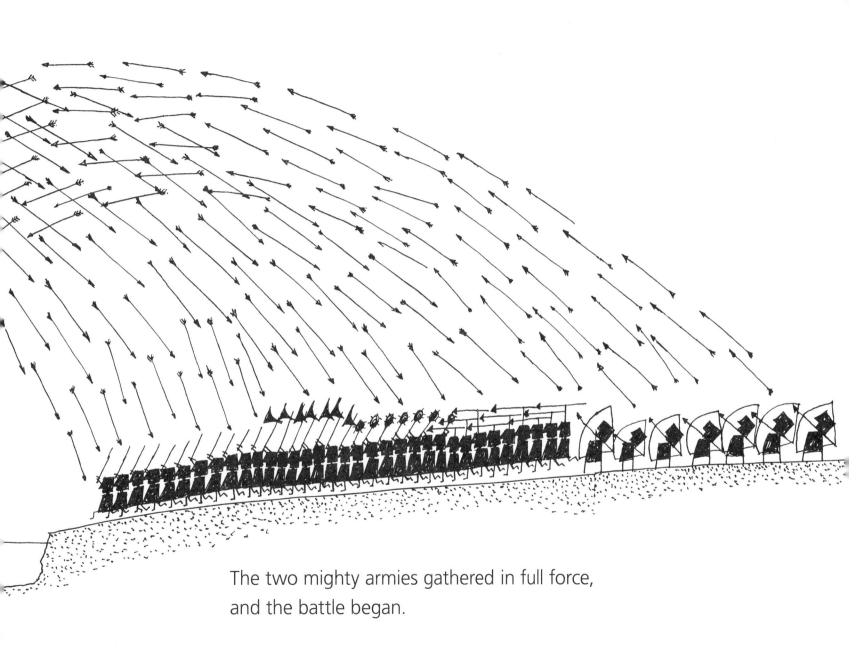

The two mighty armies gathered in full force,
and the battle began.

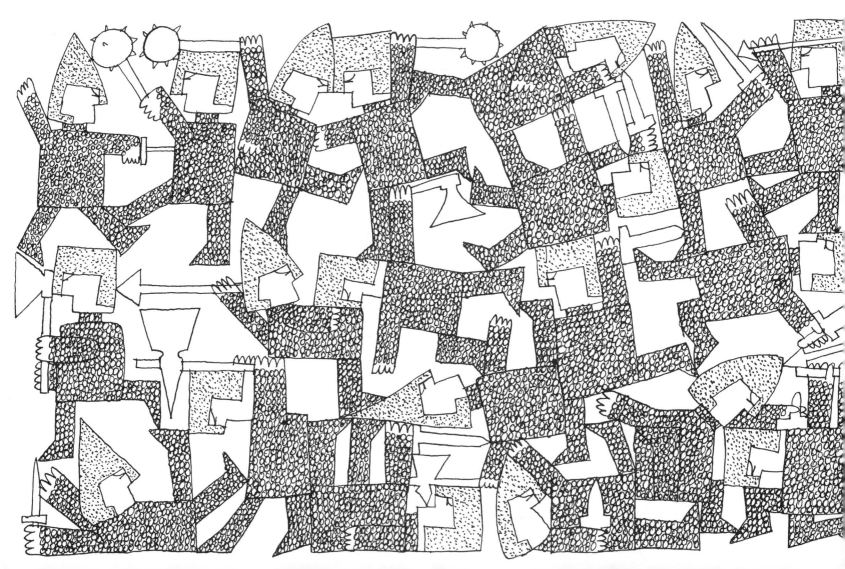

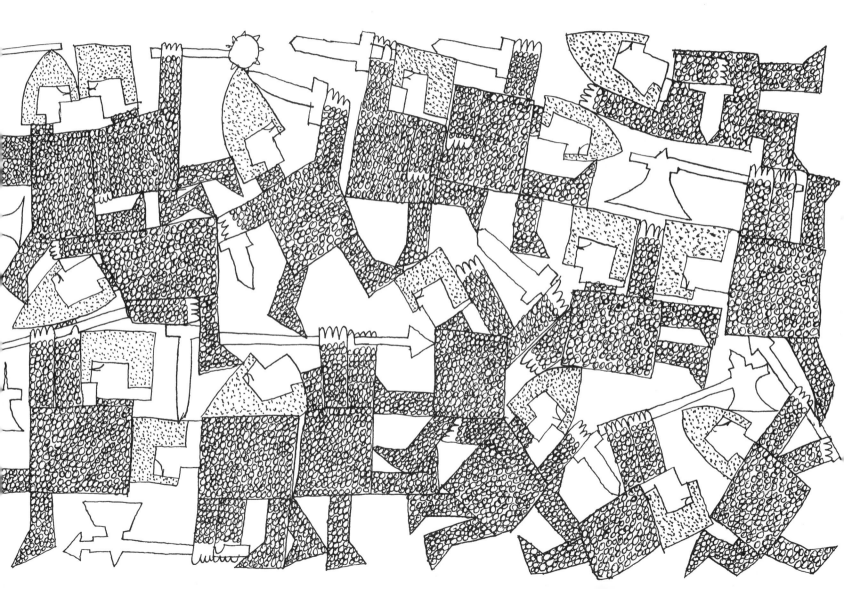

And when the battle eventually ended . . .

there was nobody left alive.

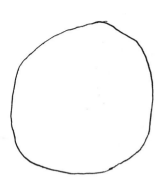

Nobody, that is, except six men from either side,
who turned their backs on one another
and started to travel the world

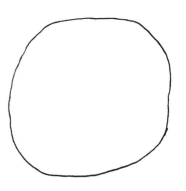

searching for a place

where they might live and work in peace.